LITTLE JAMIE BOOK

What It's Like to Be...
Qué se siente al ser...

SELENA GÓMEZ

BY/POR
JOHN BANKSTON

TRANSLATED BY/
TRADUCIDO POR
EIDA DE LA VEGA

Mitchell Lane
PUBLISHERS

P.O. Box 196
Hockessin, Delaware 19707
Visit us on the web: www.mitchelllane.com
Comments? Email us:
mitchelllane@mitchelllane.com

Mitchell Lane
PUBLISHERS

Printing   1   2   3   4   5   6   7   8   9

A LITTLE JAMIE BOOK

What It's Like to Be . . .   Qué se siente al ser . . .

América Ferrera	América Ferrera
Cameron Díaz	Cameron Díaz
George López	George López
Jennifer López	Jennifer López
The Jonas Brothers	Los Hermanos Jonas
Kaká	Kaká
Mariano Rivera	Mariano Rivera
Mark Sánchez	Mark Sánchez
Marta Vieira	Marta Vieira
Miley Cyrus	Miley Cyrus
Óscar De La Hoya	Óscar De La Hoya
Pelé	Pelé
President Barack Obama	El presidente Barack Obama
Ryan Howard	Ryan Howard
Selena Gómez	Selena Gómez
Shakira	Shakira
Sonia Sotomayor	Sonia Sotomayor
Vladimir Guerrero	Vladimir Guerrero

Library of Congress Cataloging-in-Publication Data
Bankston, John, 1974–
  What it's like to be Selena Gómez / by John Bankston ; translated by Eida de la Vega =
¿Qué se siente al ser Selena Gómez? / por John Bankston ; traducido por Eida de la Vega.
    p. cm. — (A little Jamie book = Un libro "little Jamie")
  Includes bibliographical references and index.
  ISBN 978-1-61228-321-0 (library bound)
  1. Gómez, Selena, 1992- —Juvenile literature. 2. Actors—United States—Biography—
Juvenile literature. 3. Singers—United States—Biography—Juvenile literature. I. Vega,
Eida de la. II. Title. III. Title: ¿Qué se siente al ser Selena Gómez?. IV. Title: What it's like to
be Selena Gómez.
  PN2287.G585B36 2012
  791.4302'8092—dc23
  [B]
                                                                          2012028103
eBook ISBN: 9781612283913

PUBLISHER'S NOTE: The following story has been thoroughly researched, and to the best of our knowledge represents a true story. While every possible effort has been made to ensure accuracy, the publisher will not assume liability for damages caused by inaccuracies in the data and makes no warranty on the accuracy of the information contained herein. This story has not been authorized or endorsed by Selena Gómez.

PLB

What It's Like to Be... /
Qué se siente al ser...

SELENA GÓMEZ

Selena accepts the award for Favorite TV Actress at Nickelodeon's 24th Annual Kids' Choice Awards

Selena acepta el premio a la Actriz Favorita de TV, en los XXIV Premios Anuales Kids' Choice de Nickelodeon

Nick Cannon

Heidi Klum

Award Presenters/ *Presentadores del premio*

Selena Gómez is an actress and a singer. She has been on television shows and in movies.

Selena Gómez es una actriz y cantante. Ha aparecido en programas de televisión y en películas.

Selena also plays the guitar, piano, and drums.

Selena también toca la guitarra, el piano y la batería.

6

Selena has recorded three albums with her band The Scene.

Selena ha grabado tres discos con su banda The Scene.

Ethan Roberts

Dane Forrest

Greg Garman

Joey Clement

Selena Marie Gómez was born in New York, New York on July 22, 1992. Her mother, Mandy Cornett, is Italian-American, and her father, Ricardo Gómez, is Mexican-American. Selena was named after the famous singer, Selena Quintanilla-Pérez. There is a statue of the singer in Texas that Selena Gómez has visited several times—she says it gives her good luck!

Selena Marie Gómez nació el 22 de julio de 1992, en la Ciudad de Nueva York. Su madre, Mandy Cornett, es ítaloamericana, y su padre, Ricardo Gómez, es méxicoamericano. Le pusieron Selena por una cantante famosa: Selena Quintanilla-Pérez. En Texas hay una estatua de la cantante que Selena Gómez ha visitado varias veces. ¡Dice que le da buena suerte!

Selena Quintanilla-Pérez Memorial in Corpus Christi, Texas

Monumento a Selena Quintanilla-Pérez, en Corpus Christi, Texas

Statue of Selena Quintanilla-Pérez / Estatua de Selena Quintanilla-Pérez

10

When Selena was five years old, her parents divorced and she moved with her mother to Grand Prairie, Texas. Since Selena did not grow up in New York or Los Angeles, it seemed unlikely that she would become a star.

GRAND PRAIRIE ■

Cuando Selena tenía cinco años, sus padres se divorciaron y ella se mudó con su madre a Grand Prairie, Texas. Como Selena no vivía en Nueva York ni en Los Ángeles, parecía improbable que se convirtiera en una estrella.

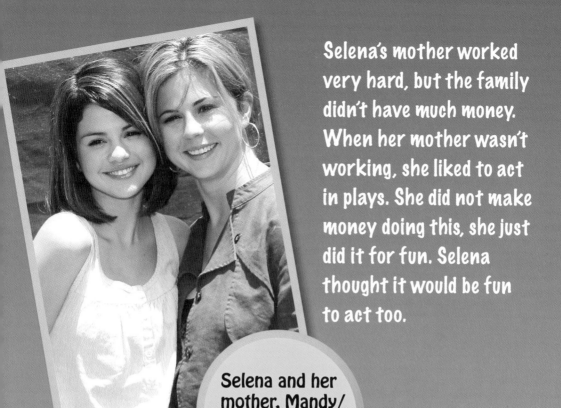

Selena's mother worked very hard, but the family didn't have much money. When her mother wasn't working, she liked to act in plays. She did not make money doing this, she just did it for fun. Selena thought it would be fun to act too.

Selena and her mother, Mandy/ *Selena y su madre, Mandy*

La mamá de Selena trabajaba muy duro, pero la familia no tenía mucho dinero. Cuando no estaba trabajando, a la mamá de Selena le gustaba actuar en obras de teatro. No le pagaban por hacerlo, pero se divertía. Selena pensó que sería divertido actuar.

The TV show *Barney & Friends* was filmed close to where Selena lived. In 1999, the show needed new performers. They let anyone who was the right age try out. These try outs are called auditions. Selena and hundreds of other young actors and actresses auditioned. Out of everyone who tried out, Selena was chosen to play Gianna!

El programa de televisión Barney y sus amigos se filmaba cerca de donde vivía Selena. En 1999, el programa necesitaba actores nuevos. Le permitieron probar suerte a todo el que tuviera la edad adecuada. Estas pruebas se llaman audiciones. Selena y cientos de otros jóvenes actores y actrices se presentaron a la audición. De todos los que se presentaron, ¡escogieron a Selena para el papel de Gianna!

BJ

Barney

Demi
Lovato

Selena
Gómez

16

Selena was on *Barney & Friends* for two years. She says it taught her a lot about what to do on a television show. Demi Lovato was on the show too, and they became best friends.

Selena estuvo dos años en Barney y sus amigos. Dice que le enseñó mucho acerca de qué hacer en un programa de televisión. Demi Lovato también estaba en el programa y se convirtieron en grandes amigas.

Selena and Demi starred together in the movie *Princess Protection Program*

Selena y Demi protagonizaron la película
Programa de Protección para Princesas

When Selena was ten, the show's producers thought she was too old, and she had to leave *Barney & Friends*. Selena was upset when they told her. She wanted to keep acting, but there were not many acting jobs in Texas. But she did find some small parts. She played the Waterpark Girl in *Spy Kids 3-D: Game Over*, which was filmed in Texas's capital, Austin.

Daryl Sabara as Juni Cortez / *Daryl Sabara como Juni Cortez*

Selena Gómez as Waterpark Girl / *Selena Gómez como Chica en el Parque Acuático*

Cuando Selena tenía diez años, los productores del programa pensaron que era demasiado mayor y tuvo que dejar Barney y sus amigos. Selena se disgustó cuando se lo dijeron. Quería seguir actuando, pero no había muchos trabajos de actuación en Texas. De todas maneras, encontró algunos papeles pequeños. Interpretó a Chica del Parque Acuático en Spy Kids 3-D: Game Over (Mini espías 3), que se filmó en Austin, la capital de Texas.

Selena
and
Minnie
Mouse

Selena y
Minnie
Mouse

In 2004, Selena Gómez's big break arrived. The Disney Channel was auditioning young actors and actresses from all over the country. They were looking for future stars who could sing as well as act. Miley Cyrus, Britney Spears, and Justin Timberlake all worked on Disney TV shows when they were younger. When the Disney Channel chose Selena, she was often compared to Miley Cyrus. Selena even appeared on three episodes of *Hannah Montana*.

Miley Cyrus

En el 2004 le llegó la gran oportunidad. El Canal Disney ofreció audiciones para jóvenes actores y actrices de todo el país. Buscaban futuras estrellas que pudiesen cantar y actuar. De pequeños, Miley Cyrus, Britney Spears y Justin Timberlake trabajaron en programas de Disney. Cuando el Canal Disney escogió a Selena, la comparaban con frecuencia con Miley Cyrus. Selena incluso apareció en tres episodios de Hannah Montana.

Selena Gómez as/*como* Alex Russo

David DeLuise as/*como* Jerry Russo

Maria Canals-Barrera as/*como* Theresa Russo

David Henrie as/*como* Justin Russo

Jake T. Austin as/*como* Max Russo

Jennifer Stone as/*como* Harper

Cast of *The Wizards of Waverly Place*/
El elenco de *Los hechiceros de Waverly Place*

In 2007, Selena starred in her very own show, Disney's *The Wizards of Waverly Place.* Her character, Alex Russo, had magical powers. Selena didn't just act on the show, she got to sing, too! She also acted in movies like *Ramona and Beezus* and *Another Cinderella Story,* where she even learned how to dance!

En el 2007, Selena protagonizó su propio programa en Disney, *Los hechiceros de Waverly Place. Su personaje, Alex Russo, tenía poderes mágicos. Selena no sólo actuó en el programa; ¡también tuvo que cantar! Además, actuó en películas como* Ramona y Beezus *y* La nueva Cenicienta, *¡donde incluso tuvo que bailar!*

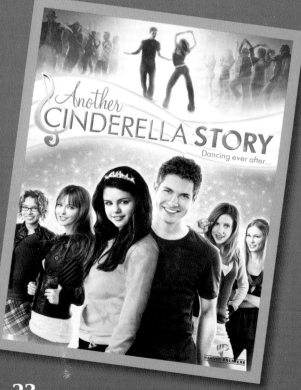

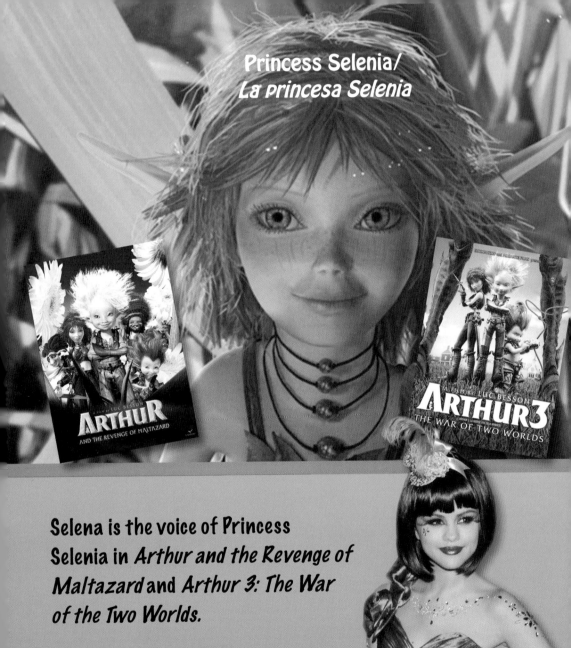

Princess Selenia/
La princesa Selenia

Selena is the voice of Princess Selenia in *Arthur and the Revenge of Maltazard* and *Arthur 3: The War of the Two Worlds.*

Selena es la voz de la princesa Selenia en Arthur y la venganza de Maltazard *y* Arthur 3: La guerra de los dos mundos.

Mavis

Selena is the voice of Mavis in the movie, *Hotel Transylvania*

Selena es la voz de Mavis en la película,
Hotel Transilvania

Selena does not just act, sing, and dance. She also likes to help others. In 2009, she became the youngest UNICEF ambassador ever. UNICEF is a group that helps poor children around the world. As a UNICEF ambassador, Selena visited places like Valparaíso, Chile where she got to see how UNICEF is helping children and families there.

Selena no sólo actúa, canta y baila. También le gusta ayudar a lo demás. En el 2009, se convirtió en la embajadora más joven que ha tenido la UNICEF. La UNICEF es un grupo que ayuda a los niño pobres del mundo. Como embajadora de la UNICEF, Selena ha visitado lugares como Valparaíso, Chile, donde vio cómo la UNICE ayudaba a niños y familias locales

Actress Selena Gomez visits Charnock Elementary School at OfficeMax's "A Day Made Better." This event donates over $1,000 of school supplies to over 1,000 teachers, and helps raise awareness about schools in need.

La actriz Selena Gómez visita la escuela primaria Charnock durante el evento de Office Max "Un día hecho mejor". Este evento proporciona a 1100 maestros más de $1000 en útiles escolares y crea conciencia sobre la necesidad de los mismos.

Selena is proud of her Hispanic heritage, and has even recorded several songs in Spanish. In 2012, she announced that she will stop working with The Scene for now. She wants to focus on becoming a better actress, and to work in more movies. Whatever is in Selena's future, she says she's thankful for all the opportunities she's already been given!

Selena holds a golden record for 30,000 records sold /
Selena tiene un disco de oro por 30.000 discos vendidos

Selena está orgullosa de sus raíces hispanas e, incluso, ha grabado varias canciones en español. En el 2012, anunció que, por el momento va a dejar de trabajar con The Scene. Quiere enfocarse en ser mejor actriz y actuar en más películas. Sea lo que sea que el futuro le depare, Selena dice que está muy agradecida por todas las oportunidades que ha tenido.

Fans from all over the world love to watch Selena perform.

A sus admiradores de todo el mundo les encanta verla en escena.

In 2011, Selena released her own perfume.

En 2011, Selena lanzó su propio perfume.

FURTHER READING/LECTURAS RECOMENDADAS

Edwards, Posy. *Selena Gomez: Me & You*. London: Orion, 2011.

Harte, Harlee. *I (Heart) Selena Gomez*. Beverly Hills: Dove, 2009.

Nelson, Maria. *Selena Gomez*. New York: Gareth Stevens Publishing, 2012.

Orr, Tamra. *Day By Day With . . . Selena Gómez*. Hockessin, DE: Mitchell Lane Publishers, 2011.

Reusser, Kayleen. *Selena Gomez*. Hockessin, DE: Mitchell Lane Publishers, 2009.

Schwartz, Heather E. *Selena Gomez*. Mankato, MN: Capstone Press, 2012.

Tieck, Sarah. *Selena Gomez*. Edina, MN: ABDO, 2009.

INTERNET SITES / SITIOS DE INTERNET:

Selena Gomez Official Web Site / Sitio oficial de Selena Gómez
http://www.selenagomez.com/

Selena Gómez Latinoamerica,
http://www.selenaonline.org/

UNICEF: Teen Sensation Selena Gomez Appointed UNICEF Ambassador /

UNICEF: Ídolo adolescente Selena Gómez nombrada embajadora de la UNICEF
http://www.unicefusa.org/news/releases/teen-sensation-selena-Gómez.html

The Wizards of Waverly Place
http://tv.disney.go.com/disneychannel/wizardsofwaverlyplace/

Los Hechiceros de Waverly Place
http://www.disneylatino.com/disneychannel/series/wizardsofwaverlyplace/

WORKS CONSULTED/ OBRAS CONSULTADAS

Etkin, Jaimie. "Good Girl Interrupted." *Newsweek*, July 11, 2011.

"From Texas to Hollywood." *People*, July 22, 2009.

"Gómez and her Band The Scene Part Ways." *World Entertainment News Network*, February 13, 2012.

"Gómez Rubs Selena's . . ." *World Entertainment News Network*, November 17, 2010.

Huff, Richard. "Selena Gómez 'learned a lot' from Barney." *New York Daily News*, October 9, 2007.
http://www.nydailynews.com/entertainment/television/selena-Gómez-learned-a-lot-barney-article-1.226639

Paton, Maureen. "Selena's Sweet Smell of Success." *The [London] Daily Mail*, June 19, 2010.

"Plus Three: Selena Gómez Reaches Facebook Fan Milestone." *Entertainment Close-up*, July 11, 2011.

"Selena to Sing in Spanish." *World Entertainment News Network*, February 14, 2011.

"Small Town Girl Makes Good." *Teen Magazine*, Fall 2008.

"Unicef Ambassador Selena Gómez Visits Chile." *PR Newswire*, February 2, 2011.

INDEX/ÍNDICE

ABOUT THE AUTHOR: Born in Boston, Massachusetts, John Bankston began writing articles while still a teenager. Since then, over 200 of his articles have been published in magazines and newspapers across the country, including travel articles in *The Tallahassee Democrat*, *The Orlando Sentinel*, and *The Tallahassean*. He is the author of over sixty biographies for young adults, including works on Drew Barrymore, Jessica Simpson, and Mandy Moore. He currently lives in Newport Beach, California and admits to sometimes listening to Selena Gómez's songs while he writes.

ACERCA DEL AUTOR: Nacido en Boston, Massachusetts, John Bankston empezó a publicar artículos de adolescente. Desde entonces, ha publicado más de 200 artículos en revistas y periódicos de todo el país, incluyendo artículos de viajes en *The Tallahassee Democrat*, *The Orlando Sentinel* y *The Tallahassean*. Es autor de más de sesenta biografías para jóvenes, que incluyen trabajos sobre Drew Barrymore, Jessica Simpson y Mandy Moore. Actualmente vive en Newport Beach, California, y admite que a veces escucha las canciones de Selena Gómez mientras escribe.

ABOUT THE TRANSLATOR: Eida de la Vega was born in Havana, Cuba, and now lives in New Jersey with her mother, her husband, and her two children. Eida has worked at Lectorum/Scholastic, and as editor of the magazine *Selecciones del Reader's Digest*.

ACERCA DE LA TRADUCTORA: Eida de la Vega nació en La Habana, Cuba, y ahora vive en Nueva Jersey con su madre, su esposo y sus dos hijos. Ha trabajado en Lectorum/Scholastic y, como editora, en la revista *Selecciones del Reader's Digest*.